AGE OF YŌKAI

Story by
Sean Meighen

Art by
Rich Perrotta

Colors by
Eugen Betivu

Letters & Logo by
Micah Myers

Chapter One

JAPAN.
SENGOKU PERIOD.

ONE HUNDRED YEARS OF CIVIL WAR HAS TORN THE COUNTRY APART.
DAIMYO AGAINST DAIMYO.
BROTHER AGAINST BROTHER.

WAR, FAMINE, EARTHQUAKES.
THE LAND OF THE RISING SUN IS SOAKED IN THE BLOOD OF ITS PEOPLE.
AND FROM THAT BLOOD... CAME THE YŌKAI.

UHNN...
GODS, NO...!
PLEASE, DO NOT BE AFRAID.

THE WORST IS NOW BEHIND YOU.

WHO... WHO ARE YOU?

YOU MAY CALL ME OSUMA. THIS IS TAICHI AND AKITO. WE ARE SAMURAI. WE SAW THE SMOKE AND CAME TO HELP. CAN YOU TELL US WHAT HAPPENED HERE?

WHAT HAPPENED...

RUN, SONOMI! RUN!

AAAAGGGH!!

YŌKAI.

THEY CAME OUT OF NOWHERE. THEY DESTROYED OUR HOME, SET FIRE TO THE VILLAGE. AND MY FATHER... THEY KILLED MY FATHER. HE WAS ALL I HAD LEFT.
WHAT IS YOUR NAME, GIRL?
SONOMI.
I AM SORRY FOR YOUR LOSS, SONOMI. WE WILL SEE TO IT YOUR FATHER — AND ALL THE PEOPLE OF THIS VILLAGE — RECEIVE PROPER BURIALS.
MORE YŌKAI ARE APPEARING EVERY DAY. ARE YOU CERTAIN THESE ARE THE SAME ONES WE HAVE BEEN TRACKING?
I'M SURE OF IT, TAICHI. WE'RE CLOSE ON THEIR TAIL. AND WE'RE GETTING CLOSER.
THEY CAN'T HAVE GOTTEN FAR.

CAAAWWWWWN
TENGUI
OSUMA! LOOK OUT!
WHACK
AAAAHH!!

UHHH!!
STRUGGLE, LITTLE SAMURAI. IT PLEASES ME TO SEE YOU SQUIRM!
GGGHHH...
SHUNK

YOU WILL JOIN YOUR MASTER SOON.

SHUCK
AAAAIIEE!!
≥COUGH COUGH≤
FOR MY FATHER.
SSSSSSSSS

THE GIRL IS STRONGER THAN SHE LOOKS.
YOUR SWORD.
THANK YOU, SONOMI.
YOU RISKED YOUR LIFE TO SAVE MINE. WHY?
I COULD NOT STAND BY AND LET IT KILL YOU. I CANNOT — WILL NOT — LET ANYONE ELSE DIE TODAY.
I AM IN YOUR DEBT.
YOU WILL COME WITH US TONIGHT AND WE WILL FIND YOU SAFE HAVEN IN THE MORNING. GATHER WHAT POSSESSIONS YOU HAVE LEFT, IF ANY. BY THE TIME THE SUN SETS, WE WILL BE RID OF THIS PLACE.
THANK YOU.
TAICHI, AKITO. HELP ME BURY THE DEAD.
OF COURSE.
AND WHO KNOWS WHAT OTHER SURPRISES STILL AWAIT US.
LET US BE PROPER, BUT LET US ALSO BE SWIFT. NIGHT IS COMING.

HERE, SONOMI, HAVE THE LAST OF THE RICE. YOU NEED TO REGAIN YOUR STRENGTH.
ARE YOU SURE? I DO NOT WANT YOU TO GO HUNGRY.
HAI! TAKE A LOOK AT ME, CHILD, AND YOU WILL SEE I HAVE NEVER GONE HUNGRY A DAY IN MY LIFE!
I CANNOT THANK YOU ENOUGH FOR LOOKING AFTER ME. WITH MY VILLAGE GONE... I FEEL I NO LONGER HAVE A PLACE IN THIS WORLD.
THEN WE ARE ALIKE IN THAT REGARD! WE'VE BEEN ROAMING THIS LAND FOR WEEKS NOW. HOME IS A CONCEPT LONG FORGOTTEN TO US.
ARE YOU ON A PILGRIMAGE? IS THAT HOW YOU FOUND MY VILLAGE?
NOT A PILGRIMAGE. A MISSION. WE HAVE BEEN TRACKING THE YŌKAI WHO ATTACKED YOUR VILLAGE. THAT IS HOW WE FOUND YOU.
ARE YOU YŌKAI SLAYERS?
WE WANT ODOKURO.
NO. THE YŌKAI ARE NOT OUR TARGETS. THEY ARE MERELY SERVANTS. WE WANT THEIR MASTER.

ODOKURO?
YOU KNOW OF HER?
I HAVE HEARD TALES OF THE LADY ODOKURO SINCE I WAS LITTLE.
AND WHAT DO THEY SAY IN THESE TALES?
THEY SAY ALL THE DAIMYO OF THIS REGION LIVE IN FEAR OF HER AND THAT NONE WHO GAZE UPON HER FACE EVER LIVE TO TELL THE TALE.
ALL TRUE.
"THAT SHE IS A WITCH AND A DEMONESS. THAT SHE FEEDS ON THE PAIN AND MISERY OF THE INNOCENT. THAT SHE COMMANDS ENTIRE LEGIONS OF YŌKAI, BUT IS WORSE THAN ANY YŌKAI HERSELF."
AND YOU MEAN TO KILL HER?
WE MEAN TO TRY.
WHY?
THAT, YOUNG SONOMI, IS A STORY IN AND OF ITSELF.

"WE WERE NOT ALWAYS THE WANDERING RONIN YOU SEE BEFORE YOU. ONCE WE WERE LOYAL SAMURAI. WE HAD A HOME. AND WE HAD A MASTER."
"OUR DAIMYO WAS A KIND AND JUST RULER. HE WEPT TO SEE THE STATE OF NIPPON AS IT IS NOW. HE DREAMT OF A LAND NO LONGER DIVIDED. A COUNTRY AT PEACE."
"HE DREAMT OF A COUNTRY UNITED."
"AS HIS LOYAL SUBJECTS, WE SHARED IN OUR MASTER'S DREAM. WE VENTURED FAR AND WIDE TO SPREAD HIS MESSAGE OF UNITY TO THE DAIMYO OF THE OTHER DOMAINS. PEACE SEEMED WITHIN OUR GRASP."

"HOW WRONG WE WERE."

ODOKURO LEARNED OF OUR MISSION, AND WAS DISPLEASED. SHE COULD NOT INSPIRE FEAR IN THE HEARTS AND MINDS OF A PEOPLE UNITED. AND SO, SHE EXPRESSED HER DISPLEASURE THE ONLY WAY SHE KNEW HOW.

"BY THE TIME THE DUST CLEARED AND THE LAST LIVING YŌKAI FLED, ONLY WE THREE WERE LEFT STANDING. WE THREE... AND OUR MASTER.

"WITH HIS DYING BREATH, OUR DAIMYO BEGGED US TO CARRY ON HIS DREAM, TO STRIVE FOR A LAND FREE OF CONFLICT AND WARFARE. HE BID US TO SERVE THE INNOCENT AND DEFEND THE JUST.

"ON HIS DEATH, WE SWORE IT."
NOW WE AIM TO AVENGE THE DEATH OF OUR MASTER, AS WELL AS ALL THOSE WE FAILED TO DEFEND. FOR SO LONG AS ODOKURO LIVES...

OUR MASTER'S DREAM CAN NEVER BE FULFILLED.

SO THE YŌKAI WHO ATTACKED MY VILLAGE...
IF ONLY WE HAD NOT BEEN SO FAR BEHIND. PERHAPS YOUR VILLAGE COULD HAVE BEEN SPARED.
WERE THE SAME WHO KILLED OUR DAIMYO. WE HAVE BEEN TRACKING THEM FOR WEEKS, HOPING THEY WILL LEAD US TO LADY ODOKURO.
DO NOT BLAME YOURSELVES. IF WHAT YOU SAY IS TRUE, THEN I KNOW WHO IS TO BLAME. THE ONE WHO COMMANDS THE YŌKAI.
ODOKURO.
DO NOT DWELL ON SUCH THINGS, SONOMI. LEAVE ODOKURO TO US. IN THE MORNING WE WILL MAKE FOR THE CLOSEST VILLAGE AND FIND SOMEONE WHO CAN TAKE YOU IN.

RUSTLE
RUSTLE
WHAT WAS THAT?
GET BEHIND US, SONOMI.
HERE IT COMES.
CAAAWWWWWN

CRAAAAWWWWW

MORE TENGU!

ENOUGH TO AVENGE THE DEATH OF OUR BROTHER!

UGH!!

HA HAHA HA!!

THE THREE OF YOU HAVE BEEN A THORN IN OUR LADY'S SIDE FOR FAR TOO LONG!
CLANG
WE ATTACKED THE VILLAGE TO DRIVE YOU OUT OF HIDING!
AND NOW HERE YOU ARE! EASY PREY!
THAT MASK...

NOT SO EASY, PERHAPS, AS YOU WERE HOPING!
WHAM
WE WILL NOT LET YOU STOP US FROM REACHING ODOKURO!
WHUMP
SCREEEEE!!
TO BELIEVE OTHERWISE...WAS FOOLISH.
I KNOW THAT YOKAI.

CRACK
SLICE
SSSSSSSSSSS
NO...

COWARD.
CLANG
CAAAWWWWWW
AND NOW, MONSTER...
YOU MEET YOUR END.
THUD

OSUMA, LEND ME YOUR BLADE ONE LAST TIME.
WAIT!
SONOMI? WHAT ARE YOU DOING?
THIS IS THE MONSTER WHO KILLED MY FATHER.
DO YOU RECOGNIZE ME, TENGU? IS MY FACE FAMILIAR TO YOU?
PLEASE. LITTLE GIRL. KIND GIRL. SHOW MERCY. SPARE ME.
ANSWER MY QUESTION! DO YOU RECOGNIZE ME?
YOU...!
ME!

THE MONSTER IS DEAD...BUT I DO NOT FEEL ANY BETTER.
BECAUSE THE CREATURE'S MASTER, ODOKURO, STILL LIVES.
SHLCK

THEN I WANT TO COME WITH YOU.

LET ME JOIN YOU ON YOUR QUEST. I DON'T CARE HOW LONG IT TAKES. I WILL HAVE JUSTICE FOR MY FATHER... AND I WILL NOT REST UNTIL LADY ODOKURO IS DEAD.

I SEE THE FIRE IN YOUR EYES. I DO NOT BELIEVE I COULD STOP YOU IF I WISHED TO.

THEN I MAY JOIN YOU?

GET SOME SLEEP, SONOMI. WE LEAVE AT DAWN. TOGETHER.

ELSEWHERE.

TO BE CONTINUED...

Chapter Two

YOU ARE CERTAIN THIS RIVER WILL LEAD US TO LADY ODOKURO'S CASTLE?
YES. THE RIVER FLOWS INTO A GREAT LAKE. HER CASTLE SITS IN THE MIDDLE OF THAT LAKE.
YOU HAVE OUR THANKS. NO ONE ELSE WOULD SPEAK TO US.
THEY ARE FRIGHTENED, AND FOR GOOD REASON. ODOKURO DEMANDS FROM US A SACRIFICE EVERY YEAR, TO ENSURE THE YŌKAI DO NOT HARM OUR VILLAGE.
"ON THE FIRST DAY OF THE FIRST MONTH, AN ARROW UNERRINGLY STRIKES ONE OF OUR HOMES. THE YOUNG-EST CHILD OF THAT HOUSE IS THEN SENT UP THE RIVER, NEVER TO BE SEEN AGAIN."
HOW HORRIBLE!
WE HAVE DONE THIS FOR LONGER THAN ANY MAN OR WOMAN CAN REMEMBER.
LAST YEAR, THE ARROW STRUCK MY HOME, AND IT WAS MY SON WHO WAS CHOSEN.
YOU SEEK TO KILL LADY ODOKURO? THEN MAY ALL THE GODS BE WITH YOU.

TO DO SUCH AN AWFUL THING, YEAR AFTER YEAR...IT IS UNTHINKABLE.
DO NOT JUDGE THEM SO HARSHLY. WE LIVE IN DARK TIMES.
PEOPLE DIE EVERY DAY. AND UNTIL WE CAN BRING OURSELVES CLOSER TOGETHER, RATHER THAN TEAR EACH OTHER APART...PEOPLE WILL ONLY CONTINUE TO DIE.
YOUR DAIMYO SOUGHT TO UNITE THE COUNTRY, DID HE NOT?
HE DID. BUT THE MORE TIME GOES BY, THE LESS LIKELY IT SEEMS NIPPON WILL EVER KNOW PEACE.
I WILL NOT GIVE UP SO EASILY.
LADY ODOKURO IS RESPONSIBLE FOR THE DEATH OF MY FATHER AND THE DESTRUCTION OF MY VILLAGE. I WILL NOT REST UNTIL I SEE HER PAY FOR HER CRIMES...OR DIE TRYING.
LET US HOPE IT DOES NOT COME TO THAT.

THAT'S ENOUGH FOR TODAY. WE WILL SET UP CAMP HERE AND SET OUT AGAIN IN THE MORNING.
I'M GOING TO WASH UP BY THE RIVER.
YOU BE CAREFUL, SONOMI. WHO KNOWS WHAT YŌKAI LURK IN THESE WOODS?
YOU WORRY TOO MUCH, TAICHI. I WILL BE FINE.

SPLOOOOSH
AAAAHHH!!

KEKEKEKEKE!!

NO! NO! LET GO!

KAKKK!!

SOMEONE! HELP!

NO!
PLEASE...
KAKKK!!
SMASH

ARE YOU HURT, SONOMI?
NO. THANK YOU, TAICHI. YOU SAVED MY LIFE.

WHAT IS IT?
A KAPPA. THEY USUALLY ONLY GO AFTER CHILDREN. THIS ONE WAS EITHER VERY BRAVE...OR VERY HUNGRY.

IT WOULD SEEM THE RIVER IS JUST AS TREACHEROUS AS THE WOODS.
PERHAPS WE SHOULD MOVE CAMP FURTHER AWAY FROM THE WATER, JUST TO BE SAFE.

ARE YOU SURE YOU ARE ALRIGHT, SONOMI? YOU'RE SHAKING.

IT WAS ALL SO FAST, OSUMA. I DIDN'T KNOW WHAT TO DO. I'VE NEVER FELT SO VULNERABLE BEFORE, SO... HELPLESS.

PERHAPS I CAN HELP YOU WITH THAT.

CLANG
CLANG
SWISH
WHAT ARE THEY DOING?
SPARRING. A SAMURAI MUST KEEP HIS SKILLS AS SHARP AS HIS BLADE. DOUBLY SO FOR US, CONSIDERING THE MAGNITUDE OF OUR MISSION.

SONOMI, I HAVE BEEN THINKING, AND I BELIEVE IT IS TIME YOU HAD A SWORD OF YOUR OWN.
AMONG OTHER THINGS, YES. YOU HAVE PROVEN YOURSELF TO BE MORE THAN MEETS THE EYE.
BECAUSE OF WHAT HAPPENED AT THE RIVER?
"OF NOBLE LINEAGE OR NOT, YOU ARE NOT MERELY THE DAUGHTER OF A SIMPLE FARMER...YOU ARE A WARRIOR BORN.
"I SAW THIS IN YOU THE VERY DAY WE MET."
YOU HAVE ENDURED MANY HARDSHIPS. YOU HAVE EVEN CHOSEN TO AID US IN OUR QUEST TO KILL LADY ODOKURO. AND YOU HAVE DONE SO BRAVELY, WITHOUT HESITATION.
EARLIER TODAY YOU TOLD ME YOU FELT VULNERABLE IN THE FACE OF DANGER. HELPLESS, EVEN. I HOPE TO RECTIFY THAT.
WITH THIS.

I RECEIVED THIS SWORD FROM MY OWN MENTOR MANY YEARS AGO, AND HAVE KEPT IT WITH ME EVER SINCE. IT IS CALLED THE TAMASHINOKEN.
THE SWORD OF SOULS.
THE SWORD CAN'T REALLY SUMMON THE SOULS OF THE DEAD...CAN IT?
I DO NOT KNOW. BUT IN TIMES SUCH AS THESE, WE ALL LOOK TO THOSE WE HAVE LOST FOR STRENGTH.
"ACCORDING TO LEGEND, THE TAMASHINOKEN WAS CRAFTED BY THE MOON GOD TSUKUYOMI HIMSELF. IT IS SAID THAT THE BLADE HAS THE POWER TO CALL FORTH THE SOULS OF DECEASED LOVED ONES IN BATTLE."
ENCHANTED OR NOT, IT IS A FINE BLADE. KEEP IT SAFE, AND IT WILL KEEP YOU SAFE.
THANK YOU, OSUMA. I WILL USE IT WELL.
TAMASHINOKEN...

LATER.
SONOMIIII...
HELLO, SONOMI.
WHAT—

WAKE UP, LITTLE FLY.
THAT'S IT. OPEN THOSE PRETTY EYES.
GODS...
WELCOME TO MY PARLOR.

SONOMI!!!
SONOMI!!! CAN YOU HEAR ME?
DAMN! WHERE COULD THAT GIRL HAVE GONE?
IF SHE RAN OFF, I WOULD HAVE HEARD HER. THERE IS SOMETHING AMISS.
YOU ARE CERTAIN YOU DID NOT SEE ANYTHING?
IF I HAD, I WOULD HAVE TOLD YOU.
THEN WE MUST ASSUME THE WORST. SONOMI HAS BEEN TAKEN IN HER SLEEP.
BUT BY WHOM? AND FOR WHAT PURPOSE?
OSUMA, AKITO. I FEAR WE HAVE OTHER PROBLEMS AT THE MOMENT.

ARE THOSE... SPIDERS?
SSSSSSSSSSSSSSSSS
IT SEEMS SONOMI WILL HAVE TO WAIT, FOR THE MOMENT.
FIRST A KAPPA, NOW WE FACE SPIDERS? ODOKURO'S REACH IS LONG, INDEED.
THEN LET'S CUT IT DOWN TO SIZE!

WHO ARE YOU? WHAT DO YOU WANT WITH ME?
I AM CALLED JOROGUMO. AND IT'S NOT WHAT I WANT WITH YOU, LITTLE FLY — IT IS WHAT MY MISTRESS, LADY ODOKURO, WANTS.
IT SEEMS YOU AND YOUR LITTLE SAMURAI HAVE BECOME QUITE THE NUISANCE TO MY LADY. AS HER LOYAL SERVANT, IT IS MY DUTY TO...REMOVE SUCH NUISANCES.
YOU SHOULD BE FLATTERED, LITTLE FLY. USUALLY IT IS HANDSOME YOUNG MEN WHO ARE MY PREY.
OH, HOW I DO ENJOY A DELICIOUS YOUNG MAN!
BUT A SUBJECT MUST SERVE HER MISTRESS...AND A MOTHER MUST FEED HER CHILDREN.

THEN YOUR CHILDREN WILL GO HUNGRY TONIGHT! I AM NO LOVESTRUCK FOOL.
SLAAAASH
NO!!
I AM A WARRIOR!
AND I WILL NOT DIE WITHOUT A FIGHT!

SCREEEEEEEE

WE CAN'T KEEP THIS UP FOREVER! WE HAVE TO FIND SONOMI!!

TELL THAT TO THE SPIDERS. THERE IS NO END TO THEM!

CRUNCH

WHEREVER YOU ARE, SONOMI... I PRAY YOU ARE DOING BETTER THAN WE.

YOU YŌKAI ARE ALL THE SAME. YOU THINK I'M JUST SOME HELPLESS LITTLE GIRL.

WHY ELSE WOULD YOU HAVE BEEN *FOOLISH* ENOUGH TO LEAVE MY SWORD WITHIN ARM'S REACH?

THE BLADE WAS TO BE A TROPHY FOR MY MISTRESS.

BUT NOW, I THINK, YOUR HEAD WILL MAKE A MUCH BETTER GIFT!

CLANG

UNGH!!

HSSSSSSS
NO! I WON'T BE YOUR VICTIM!
I WILL NEVER BE ANYONE'S VICTIM EVER AGAIN!
AAAAIIIEEE!!
SLASH

SHWAAAK
THUMP
HUH... HUH... HUH...
LADY ODOKURO IS MORE POWERFUL THAN YOU CAN IMAGINE. YOU WILL FALL BEFORE HER...AND SHE WILL PEEL THE FLESH FROM YOUR BONES.
THIS ISN'T OVER. NOT FOR YOU.
WE'LL SEE.

SHUK'K
THERE ARE TOO MANY OF THEM, OSUMA! WE'LL BE OVERRUN!
THEN WE WILL DO SO WITH HONOR... AND KILL AS MANY AS WE CAN BEFORE WE FALL!
SCREEEEEEEEE
WHAT...?

THEY... FLED, ALL OF THEM.
BUT WHY?

BECAUSE THE VOICE OF THEIR MOTHER FELL SILENT.

SONOMI! WHERE HAVE YOU BEEN?
IN THE LAIR OF THE JOROGUMO. SHE ABDUCTED ME UNDER ORDERS FROM LADY ODOKURO. SHE THOUGHT I WOULD BE EASY PREY.

AND I SAW TO IT THEY WILL NEVER HEAR IT AGAIN.

SHE WAS WRONG.

I AM GLAD TO SEE YOU ARE SAFE, SONOMI. I TRUST THE TAMASHINOKEN SERVED YOU WELL?
IT DID. IT MAY NOT HAVE SUMMONED THE SPIRITS OF MY ANCESTORS... BUT IT CERTAINLY GAVE ME THE STRENGTH TO FIGHT BACK.
WE'VE ALL HAD A LONG NIGHT, BUT THE THREAT IS NOW PAST. TOMORROW, WE WILL CONTINUE OUR JOURNEY TO FIND LADY ODOKURO.
IN THE MEANTIME...IT'S TIME WE FINALLY GOT SOME REST.
REST?
I CAN'T REST, NOT YET.
YOU HAD YOUR CHANCE TO KILL ME, ODOKURO. YOU FAILED.
NOW IT'S MY TURN.
FWOOSH
TO BE CONTINUED...

Chapter Three

WE'RE GETTING CLOSE.

THANK THE GODS. I DON'T LIKE IT OUT HERE. THIS FOG FEELS... UNNATURAL.
IT IS. IT'S A MIASMA, NO DOUBT CONJURED UP BY ODOKURO HERSELF TO IMPEDE OUR PROGRESS.
THIS IS ODOKURO'S REALM, WHERE HER POWER IS AT ITS PEAK.
NOT EVEN THE LIGHT OF THE MOON CAN PENETRATE THIS DARKNESS.
I WON'T LET IT STOP ME. NOT ALL OF ODOKURO'S VILE YŌKAI... AND CERTAINLY NOT A LITTLE MIST. FOR MY FATHER— AND FOR YOUR MASTER— ODOKURO WILL DIE THIS NIGHT.
HA! YOU FEEL THE FIRE IN HER WORDS? THE GIRL HAS GROWN FIERCE!
TAICHI IS RIGHT. HAD YOU BEEN BORN INTO ONE OF THE HIGHER CLASSES, I HAVE NO DOUBT YOU WOULD HAVE MADE A FINE SAMURAI, SONOMI.
THANK YOU. BOTH OF YOU.

SONOMI, YOU SEEM TROUBLED.

WHAT IS WRONG?

LEGEND SAYS THE TAMASHINOKEN HAS THE POWER TO SUMMON THE SPIRITS OF THE DEAD. THAT IS WHAT YOU TOLD ME. BUT I DON'T KNOW IF I BELIEVE IT.

"WHEN I FACED THE JORŌGUMO, I THOUGHT PERHAPS THE SPIRIT OF MY FATHER WOULD APPEAR TO AID ME. BUT IT DIDN'T. I FOUGHT THE YŌKAI — AND I SLEW IT — BUT I DID SO ALONE."

SO I WONDER. IN THE FINAL BATTLE, WILL MY FATHER'S SPIRIT BE THERE? WILL I FACE ODOKURO WITH MY FATHER AT MY SIDE? OR WILL I BE ALONE ONCE AGAIN?

WE THREE WILL BE THERE WITH YOU. AKITO, TAICHI...AND MYSELF. THIS I SWEAR. WE WILL BE THERE.

ONE WAY OR ANOTHER.

I DO NOT HAVE THE ANSWERS YOU SEEK, SONOMI. BUT I DO KNOW THAT WHEN YOU FACE LADY ODOKURO... YOU WILL NOT DO SO ALONE.

OSUMA. SONOMI, LOOK AHEAD.
WE'RE HERE.
UNBELIEVABLE...

STAY CLOSE. ALL OF YOU.
THE GATE... IT'S OPEN. UNGUARDED.
IT SEEMS WE ARE EXPECTED.

IF WE GO FORWARD, WE DO SO TOGETHER. WITHOUT DOUBT, WITHOUT HESITATION.
WE'RE WITH YOU, OSUMA.
TO THE VERY END.
GOOD.
THEN FOR OUR MASTER, FOR SONOMI'S FATHER, AND FOR ALL WHO HAVE FALLEN BEFORE THE MIGHT OF THE YŌKAI... WE WILL HAVE OUR VENGEANCE.
CRACK
CRACK
WHAT WAS THAT?

CRACK
CRACK
CRACK
CRACK
OSUMA...!
STAY BEHIND US, SONOMI.
ROOOAAARRGGHH!!
CROOOOOM
ONI!
AKITO, TAICHI, TO THE LEFT! SONOMI, WITH ME!

WHAMM
CROOM
SONOMI!
NOW!
RRAARRGH!!
SLASH

ROOOAAARRGGHH!!
CLANG

ERRRRRR...
HA!
RRAAAAGGHH!!
BACK!!

SLASH
HN!
DIIIIEEE!!
AKITO! BEHIND YOU!
EH?
NO!

WHRAAM
AKITO!!

UCH!!

I WILL SEE YOU IN HELL, MONSTER.

CRUNCH

NOOO!!

SONOMI... HEAD FOR THE GATE. I WILL COVER YOU.
HA! HA! HA! HA! HA!
NO, OSUMA! YOU CAN'T FIGHT BOTH OF THEM!
I DO NOT INTEND TO FIGHT THEM.

THIS IS A POWERFUL EXPLOSIVE. IT WILL BE MORE THAN ENOUGH TO TAKE CARE OF THE ONI.
WHAT? WHY DIDN'T YOU USE IT BEFORE?!
NO?
BECAUSE IT IS A WEAPON OF LAST RESORT. FOR THE EXPLOSIVE TO WORK...IT MUST BE DETONATED BY HAND.

IT'S UP TO YOU NOW. ENTER THE CASTLE. FIND ODOKURO. END THIS NIGHTMARE ONCE AND FOR ALL!
IT IS THE ONLY WAY, SONOMI!
NO! I WON'T LEAVE YOU! I CAN'T LET YOU DO THIS!

GO!!
HURRAAGGHH!!
DAMN YOU, OSUMA...
FOR AKITO. FOR TAICHI.
FOR MY MASTER.
CLICK

UHN!

KABOOOOM
OSUMA!!

NOT AGAIN...

NO!
PLEASE, NO...
OSUMA...
YOU SAID WE WOULD FACE ODOKURO TOGETHER. YOU SAID YOU WOULD BE THERE FOR ME— ALL OF YOU. YOU SWORE IT TO ME.
YOU LIED.

CREEEAAAK
COME IN, SONOMI...
I'VE BEEN EXPECTING YOU.

YOU WILL PAY FOR THE DEATHS OF MY FRIENDS.
WILL I? YOU WILL HAVE TO FIND ME FIRST.
YOU CAN'T HIDE FROM ME, ODOKURO!
THAT'S IT, SONOMI. CLOSER. CLOSER.
NO ONE IS HIDING, SONOMI.
I'VE BEEN WITH YOU EVERY STEP OF THE WAY.

ODOKURO...
I REALLY MUST CONGRATULATE YOU, SONOMI, YOU ARE THE FIRST MORTAL TO MAKE IT THIS FAR INTO MY ABODE. TRUE, YOU HAD SOME HELP... BUT IN THE END, HERE YOU ARE, ALONE.
YOU ARE A MONSTER! MY FRIENDS DIED SO I COULD BE HERE.
AND WERE THEIR DEATHS WORTH IT, SONOMI?
YOURS WILL BE!
SO FULL OF RAGE. I'VE BEEN WATCHING YOU, YOU KNOW. THROUGH THE EYES OF MY YŌKAI I HAVE SEEN YOU FIGHT AND KILL. YOU HAVE GROWN STRONG...AS HAS YOUR THIRST FOR VENGEANCE.
IT'S NOT VENGEANCE I AM AFTER, ODOKURO. IT'S JUSTICE! JUSTICE FOR MY FATHER, FOR MY VILLAGE. JUSTICE FOR MY FRIENDS! AND I WILL NOT LEAVE THIS PLACE UNTIL JUSTICE HAS BEEN DONE!
BUT, MY DEAR SONOMI, YOU WILL NEVER LEAVE THIS PLACE.

I APPLAUD YOUR TENACITY, BUT IT WILL DO YOU NO GOOD. YOU ASSUME THAT I AM MORTAL, THAT I CAN DIE. BUT I CANNOT. INDEED, I FEAR YOUR PREVIOUS ASSESSMENT WAS THE MOST CORRECT.
I AM A MONSTER.
I AM PAIN. I AM ANGUISH. I AM THE EMBODIMENT OF ALL THAT IS WRONG WITH THIS LAND.
"NIPPON HAS BEEN AT WAR FOR A HUNDRED YEARS. IT BLEEDS, AND ITS PEOPLE BLEED WITH IT. I AM THE MANIFESTATION OF THAT SORROW."
"SOLDIERS, ORPHANS, VICTIMS OF FAMINE. I AM COMPOSED OF ALL THOSE WHO DIED WITH ANGER AND HATRED IN THEIR HEARTS. I AM A STORM COME TO WASH AWAY THE CRIMES OF YOUR PEOPLE."
I AM ODOKURO...AND I AM A GRUDGE AGAINST THE LIVING.

MORTAL OR NOT, I WILL HAVE JUSTICE! FOR ALL THOSE WHO HAVE DIED BY YOUR HAND...I SWEAR I WILL STRIKE YOU DOWN!
SHOW ME, SONOMI. SHOW ME YOUR RAGE. SHOW ME YOUR FURY. STRIKE ME DOWN...AND LET US SEE WHICH OF US IS GREATER.
SHLLUCK

"HEHEHEHE..."
HAHAHAHAHAHAHA!!
POOR SONOMI, LONELY SONOMI, YOU ARE BUT A MERE GIRL, ARMED WITH A MAGIC SWORD THAT DOES NOT WORK. BUT I TOLD YOU BEFORE...I AM SOMETHING MORE.
NOW YOU WILL BE THE FIRST TO GAZE UPON MY TRUE FORM!

I AM PAIN!
I AM ANGUISH!
BY THE GODS...
I AM GASHADOKURO!!
TO BE CONTINUED...

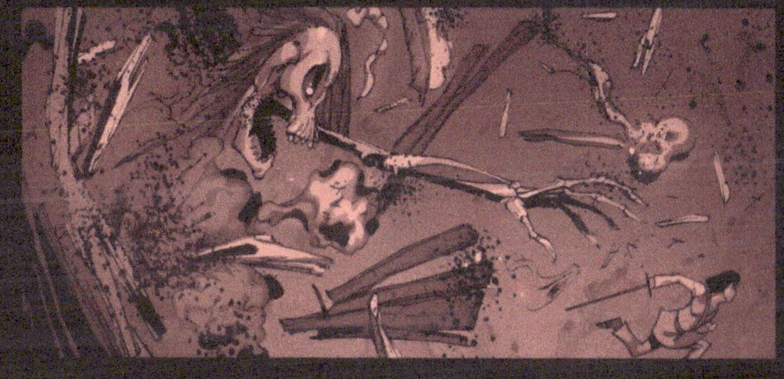

Chapter Four

"WAR.
"FAMINE.
"NATURAL DISASTERS.
"FOR OVER A HUNDRED YEARS, NIPPON HAS BEEN IN CONSTANT TURMOIL, CIVIL WAR TEARS THE COUNTRY APART. THOUSANDS DIE BY THE DAY."

"ALL THAT PAIN, ALL THAT DEATH, IT POISONS THE VERY LAND ITSELF...AND GIVES BIRTH TO MONSTERS.
"THE PAIN IN THOSE BONES--THAT MALICE-- BECOMES A LIVING, BREATHING THING.
"A FORCE OF NATURE.
"SOME ANGUISH NEVER FADES. SOME DIE WITH SO MUCH PAIN AND HATRED IN THEIR HEARTS THAT IT SEEPS INTO THEIR VERY BONES. FLESH ROTS AND BODIES DECAY...BUT THE BONES REMAIN.
"A GRUDGE AGAINST THE LIVING."

I DO NOT MERELY FEED ON THE ANGUISH OF NIPPON...
I AM THAT ANGUISH!
HAHAHAHAHAHAHAHA!!!

RUN, LITTLE SONOMI! RUN! THERE IS NOWHERE YOU CAN GO!
CROOOOM
YOU CAME SEARCHING FOR VENGEANCE. FOR JUSTICE, YOU SAID.
BUT ALL YOU WILL FIND HERE IS DEATH!

KRAKOOM
CROOSH
NOT YET...
JUST A LITTLE FARTHER...
NOW.

YOU FINALLY STOP RUNNING.
AH, THIS IS WHERE YOUR FRIENDS FOUGHT AND DIED. MY ONI WERE TOO STRONG FOR THEM. A PITY.
I SEE NOW, SONOMI, YOU CAME OUT HERE TO BE AMONG THE CORPSES OF YOUR FRIENDS. YOU WISH TO DIE HERE AS WELL, IS THAT IT?
NO, GASHADOKURO. I DIDN'T COME OUT HERE TO DIE WITH MY FRIENDS...
I CAME OUT HERE SO I COULD HAVE ROOM TO FIGHT!

EH?
SLASH
SHWAAAAK
WHACK
FOOLISH GIRL. YOUR BLADE IS AS NOTHING TO ME!

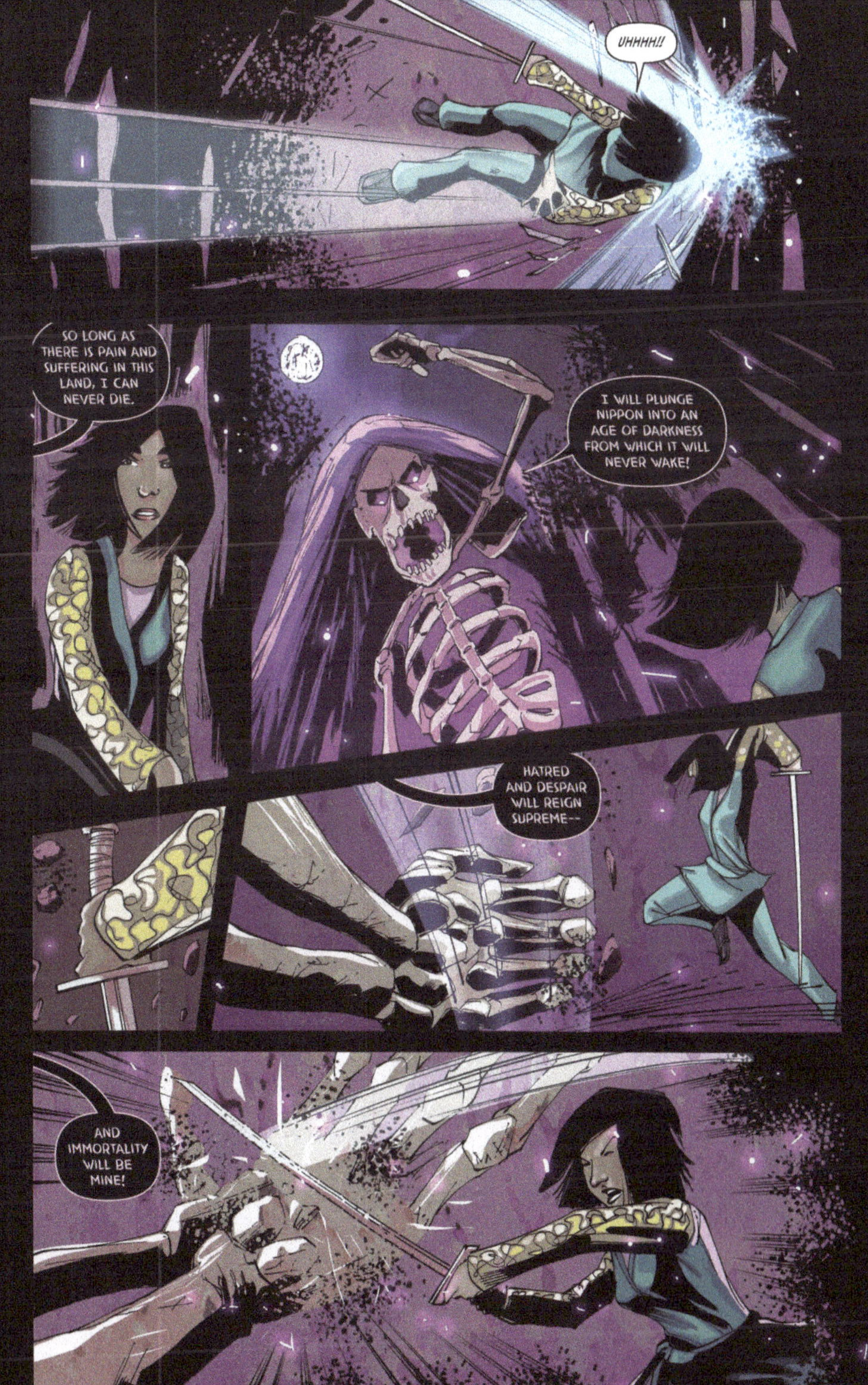

UHHHH!!
SO LONG AS THERE IS PAIN AND SUFFERING IN THIS LAND, I CAN NEVER DIE.
I WILL PLUNGE NIPPON INTO AN AGE OF DARKNESS FROM WHICH IT WILL NEVER WAKE!
HATRED AND DESPAIR WILL REIGN SUPREME--
AND IMMORTALITY WILL BE MINE!

WHACK
UUUNH!!
TAKE SOLACE, SONOMI, THAT YOU WILL NOT LIVE TO SEE THE AGE WHICH IS TO COME.
THE AGE...OF YOKAI!
OSUMA. FATHER. SOMEONE.
PLEASE...

WHAT IS THIS?!
SLASH
IT CAN'T BE. IT CAN'T BE...
ONE WAY OR ANOTHER.
WOOSH
I SWORE YOU WOULD NOT FACE ODOKURO ALONE, SONOMI. I SWORE WE WOULD BE HERE WITH YOU.

OSUMA. IT'S YOU. IT'S REALLY YOU.
YES.

AND I DO NOT COME ALONE.

SHWAAAK
AAAIIEE!!

WE GAVE OUR WORD WE WOULD BE WITH YOU UNTIL THE VERY END, SONOMI.
AND WE ALWAYS KEEP OUR WORD.

YOU CAME. I NEEDED YOU... AND YOU CAME.
THAT IS THE POWER OF THE TAMASHINOKEN. IT SUMMONS THE SOULS OF THE DEAD...TO GIVE STRENGTH TO THE LIVING.
YOU HAVE FOUGHT LONG AND HARD, SONOMI. NOW...IT IS OUR TURN.
COME THEN, LITTLE SAMURAI.
LET US SEE IF YOU CAN DIE A SECOND TIME!
AAAAAAAAAAAAAAAAA!!!

SONOMI. MY DEAR, STRONG SONOMI.
FATHER...?
FATHER! YOU'RE ALIVE!
NO, DAUGHTER, I AM DEAD AND GONE. BUT YOU ARE NOT. YOU STILL HAVE HOPE. AND SO LONG AS YOU DO...YOU CAN NEVER GIVE UP.
KRAAAAGHH!!!
THERE IS A FIRE IN YOU, SONOMI, AND IT BURNS BRIGHTER THAN THE SUMMER SUN. BUT YOU CANNOT LET IT CONSUME YOU. YOU MUST USE IT. YOU MUST BELIEVE IN YOURSELF, SONOMI—
JUST AS ALL OF US BELIEVE IN YOU.

FWOOOSH

YOU DISAPPOINT ME, LITTLE SAMURAI. EVEN SUMMONED FROM BEYOND THE GRAVE, YOU LACK THE STRENGTH TO DEFEAT ME.

THAT'S BECAUSE THEY AREN'T HERE TO DEFEAT YOU, GASHADOKURO—

EH?

I AM.

I SPENT ALL THIS TIME HATING YOU, GASHADOKURO. YOU SPREAD WAR AND FAMINE BECAUSE YOU THINK THAT'S ALL THERE IS. BUT YOU'RE WRONG. THERE IS MORE TO LIFE THAN MISERY AND FEAR.
THERE IS LOVE.
BUT YOU WILL NEVER UNDERSTAND THOSE THINGS, GASHADOKURO. YOU'RE NOT HUMAN. YOU'RE YŌKAI.
THERE IS FRIENDSHIP.
AND YOUR 'AGE OF YŌKAI' ENDS NOW!

AAAAAIIIEEE!!
VRGGGM
IT CANNOT BE...!

THE SPIRITS OF MY FRIENDS AND FAMILY ARE HERE TO GIVE ME STRENGTH. TO GIVE ME HOPE!

BUT I WILL NOT LET YOU TAKE AWAY MY HOPE!
YOU HAVE TAKEN EVERYTHING ELSE FROM ME, GASHADOKURO—

NOOOOOOO!!

HUH...
HUH...
HUH...

IT IS
DONE.

OSUMA, TAICHI, AKITO...I CAN'T THANK YOU ENOUGH. YOU TOOK ME IN, GUIDED ME, PROTECTED ME. AND IN THE END...YOU DIED FOR ME. I AM SO SORRY.
I ALWAYS HOPED I WOULD DIE IN BATTLE.
AND I, AMONG FRIENDS. IT SEEMS WE BOTH GOT OUR WISH.
YOU SEE, SONOMI, NOTHING IS AMISS.
WE LIVED. WE DIED. AND WE DID SO TOGETHER. IT IS JUST AS OUR FORMER MASTER TAUGHT US. INDIVIDUALLY, WE ARE STRONG, BUT TOGETHER, UNITED...NOTHING CAN DEFEAT US.
NOW, WITH ODOKURO DEAD, IT IS TIME ALL OF NIPPON LEARNED THIS LESSON.
AND THERE IS NO ONE MORE SUITED TO THE TASK THAN MY DAUGHTER.
I ALWAYS KNEW YOU WERE SPECIAL, SONOMI. BUT TO SEE YOU NOW, TO SEE HOW STRONG YOU HAVE BECOME...I COULD NOT BE MORE PROUD.
FATHER...

CAN'T YOU STAY?
THIS LAND IS FOR THE LIVING, AND WE ARE NO LONGER AMONG THE LIVING. WE MUST GO BEFORE THE LIGHT OF DAY FINDS US HERE.
THE CURSE PLACED UPON NIPPON HAS BEEN LIFTED WITH ODOKURO'S DEATH, BUT THAT DOES NOT MEAN THE COMING AGE WILL BE EASY. IT IS FOR YOU NOW TO GUIDE THE PEOPLE OF THIS LAND, SONOMI.
I KNOW YOU WILL MAKE US PROUD.
THANK YOU, SONOMI...AND GOODBYE.
GOODBYE...

SHUCK
THE END.